100 Puzzles, Clues, Maps, Tantalizing Tales, and Stories of Real Treasure

A Treasure's Trove
Puzzle Book Companion

By Michael Stadther

A Treasure's Trove
Puzzle Book Companion

Treasure Trove, Inc.

To Norman, Bob and all my friends who tolerated me while I was planning this project.

Printed in the United States by Treasure Trove, Inc.

Visit www.atreasurestrove.com
for information on the treasure hunt and rules and regulations of the hunt

Puzzle Book Companion
ISBN 0-9760618-1-3

Second Edition

Contents

INTRODUCTION

I wrote the 'Treasure's Trove Companion' book to get you thinking about treasures and treasure hunting. I also want you to get used to seeing things that you wouldn't ordinarily see – like the clues that I hid in the fairy tale, A Treasure's Trove, that will lead you to twelve beautiful jewels.
'A Treasure's Trove' begins...

...concealed in the pages of this story, are the clues to twelve very real and very valuable treasures that I have hidden for you to find and keep—treasures similar to the jeweled Forest Creatures in the Fairy Tale. I have selected these treasures from all around the world, and I think that they are all beautiful. I have not hidden them in remote locations, but rather I have hidden them in places accessible to everyone. You might even find one by accident, as you walk across a field or down a street. But none are on private property and none are buried. Nothing needs to be lifted or moved for you to find them. But I have hidden them well.

A Treasure's Trove is a sweet fairy tale that I wrote about good fairies and bad fairies and how a group of forest creatures combined forces with a handsome woodcarver and his beautiful wife to rescue their missing mates.

But the story is more than just a fairy tale. It is a true story in the sense that it's about treasure—over $1,000,000 in real treasure that I have hidden in twelve separate locations throughout the United States.

I have thought about treasure since I was a child when I dug holes in my grandmother's back yard, hoping to find buried treasure. As a young man, I was fascinated when I read the book, *Masquerade*, by Kit Williams which told a surreal story about a hare, the sun and the moon. In the book, Kit promised everyone that he had hidden clues in his story that they led to a wonderful golden hare. And he did as he promised. And the golden hare was found, buried in Amphill Park in England. I thought the whole idea was wonderful. And, I thought that one day, I would write a story and hide a treasure, too. But I wanted a big treasure hunt with lots of treasures and lots or opportunity for everyone.

But there were a few problems with my idea. First, I needed a million dollars to buy all of the treasure and, second, I needed the time to write and illustrate a story. Not to mention that I had to figure out how to hide the treasures and create the clues.

So, I spent the next 25 years trying to figure out how to hide treasures so that:
- They weren't on private property,
- No one else was involved,
- They weren't hidden in dangerous locations,
- They could really be found,
- And I wouldn't get sued in the process of people looking for them.

Kit had a very simple solution – he buried his treasure. It was a good technique and one that pirates had used for years. But Kit's treasure hunt took place back in the 1970's and, in today's litigious society, I had to find a better way than sending countless people out to dig up America.
Then, a few years back, all of these problems were solved. I figured out how to hide the treasure and I was fortunate enough to own and run several successful companies that, through a lot of hard work and with the help of some very bright people, brought me the financial resources that I needed to buy the treasures.

Now, I am passing some of those riches and the fun to you.

By reading 'A Treasure's Trove' and this Puzzle Companion, you will be prepared to find these treasures.

However, I haven't made it too easy and, if by chance you don't find one of the jewels, then I hope you get as much enjoyment from reading my fairy tale and looking for clues as I did years ago. It was a treasure for me then, and it will be your treasure today.

Michael Stadther

How to Use This Book

All the puzzles and illusions in this book relate in some way to solving the clues in 'A Treasures Trove'. Some puzzles and illusions will point you directly to techniques that I used in the story; others will just get you thinking like a treasure hunter.

Also, don't worry if you can't solve some of the puzzles -- not solving one may not stop you from finding the treasure.

The stories, puzzles and illusions are all prepared by me for you to solve and share with your family or your children. Most of the stories and puzzles are good for almost all ages. And, please don't think that the puzzles are only for the highly intelligent people. Rather, the puzzles in this book are not meant to be an intelligence test; they just show a different way to look at the world, a way to see things that you may have not seen before, a way to see things that were all the time right in front of you.

For example, can you see the name of an animal in the shapes below?

Look at it carefully. I promise that is not difficult and its right before your eyes.
Most people can't see it right away but once you stop looking at the shapes and look at the space between them you may see the word: CAT. (If, however, you still don't see it, the answer is at the bottom of this section.)

It was there all along -- right in front you!

Now, I won't overstate the importance of the 'Puzzle Companion' – it won't guarantee that you will find the jewels that I have hidden; but I do promise that it will help.

I've also included some stories about real treasures from around the world. Yes, there are still undiscovered, valuable treasures waiting to be found!

Finally, I've included a little information about ciphers. Ciphers are ways of concealing the meaning of written information from all but the author of the information.

While the Cipher section may be a little too complex for some people, you should at least figure out that the map to a treasure may be written in a language that only the person who hides the treasure can understand – and you may have to do a little work to decipher the clues.

But no matter whether you find one of the treasures or not, the best way to use this book is to have fun reading about treasures and solving the puzzles.

Answer:

TREASURE STORIES

THE LOST DUTCHMAN MINE

The rough Superstition Mountains, located just east of Phoenix, Arizona have been a source of mystery ever since the Peralta family of northern Mexico supposedly developed rich gold mines in the mountains in the 1840's.

Since then, a number of other people were supposed to have known the mine's location or even to have worked it. Numerous maps have surfaced over the years, only to become lost or misplaced. Many people who claimed to have found the Peralta mine were unable to return to it or some disaster occurred before they could file a claim.

In the 1870's, Jacob Waltz, "the Dutchman" was said to have located the mine through the help of one of the Peralta descendants. Waltz and his partner, Jacob Weiser, worked the mine and allegedly hid their gold in the Superstitions in the vicinity of Weaver's Needle, a well known landmark.

Jacob Waltz moved to Phoenix and died twenty years later in 1891. In failing health, he supposedly described the mine's location to Julia Thomas, a neighbor who took care of him just prior to his death. Neither she nor hundreds of other seekers in the years that followed were able to find the "Lost Dutchman's Mine."

In 1952, the "Peralta" stone tablet maps were discovered in the foothills of the Superstition Mountains by a man on vacation with his family. The stone maps are reported to be over 100 years old.

Some of the codes and symbols on the tablets are believed to show the beginning and end of the trail that leads to the Dutchman's Mine.

The intriguing search for gold mines and buried treasures has been going on for over 100 years in the Superstition Mountains of Arizona—will the mystery ever be solved?

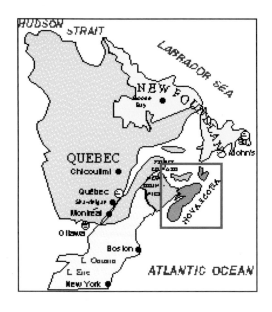

In 1795, on Oak Island, in Nova Scotia, Daniel McGinnis noticed a tree with one limb sawed off and a depression in the ground underneath. Underneath the sawed limb, it looked as if something were buried. Having heard tales of pirates in the area, he decided to return home to get friends and return to investigate.

Over the next several days McGinnis and his friends, John Smith and Anthony Vaughan, worked the area. To their astonishment, two feet below the surface they came across of layer of flagstones blocking their way. At 10 feet down they found a layer of oak logs. Again, at 20 feet and 30 feet they found more logs. At this point, they abandoned their search.

It took the trio 8 years to return. They soon dug back to the 30 foot level that had been reached 8 years ago and they continued down to 90 feet, finding a layer of oak logs at every 10 feet. At 40 feet, a layer of charcoal was found, at 50 feet a layer of putty, and at 60 feet a layer of coconut fiber.

At 90 feet, they found a stone inscribed with mysterious writing.

After pulling up the layer of oak at 90 feet, water began to seep into the pit. By the next day, the pit was filled with water up to the 33 foot level. All attempts to pump the water failed. The next year, a new pit was dug down 100 feet parallel to the original and then connected to the 'Money Pit'. Water flooded both pits and the search was abandoned for 45 years.

The group had inadvertently unplugged a 500 foot underground waterway that had been dug from the pit to nearby Smith's Cove by the pit's designers. As quickly as the water could be pumped out, it was refilled by the sea.

In 1849, The Truro Company attempted to extract the treasure by drilling core samples and, reportedly, brought up three small gold chain links on the drill bit.

In 1893, Fred Blair, along with a group called The Oak Island Treasure Company began their search. During their drilling, they found attached to their auger a small piece of sheep-skin parchment with the letters "vi"; "ui"; or "wi".

Over the next several years, different companies tried to crack the mystery unsuccessfully.

Daniel Blankenship began his quest in 1965. Blankenship found a hand-wrought nail and a washer.

Later, a pair of wrought-iron scissors was discovered in 1967 at Smith's Cove. It was deter-mined that the scissors were Spanish-American, probably made in Mexico, and were over 300 years old. He also found a heart shaped stone.

To this day, people are still trying to reach the treasure in the bottom of The Money Pit.

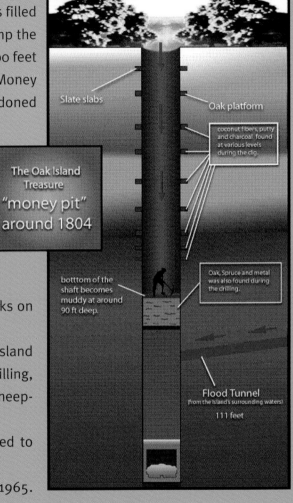

Slate slabs

Oak platform

coconut fibers, putty and charcoal, found at various levels during the dig.

The Oak Island Treasure
"money pit"
around 1804

botttom of the shaft becomes muddy at around 90 ft deep.

Oak, Spruce and metal was also found during the drilling.

Flood Tunnel
(from the island's surrounding waters)
111 feet

The stone found at the 90 foot level in the Money Pit was reportedly recorded and translated by a halifax University language professor around 1866 as "Forty Feet below two million pounds are buried".

According to the professor, a simple substitution cipher where each unique symbol corresponds to a letter in the alphabet. The key to deciphering the inscrption is:

Using this key, the words on the stone are:

Unfortunately the stone has since disappeared.

THE BEALE CIPHERS

The Beale ciphers are a set of three codes, one of which allegedly explains the location of a buried treasure of gold and silver estimated by some to be worth over 30 million dollars today.

The other two ciphers describe the content of the treasure and list the names of the original owners' next of kin.

The gold and silver in the treasure was said to have been mined around 1818 somewhere in the American Southwest by a group of adventurers led by a man named Thomas Beale.

The men decided to move their horde by wagon back to Virginia. They reportedly brought it back in two shipments and buried the gold in iron pots in a secret vault lined with stone approximately six feet beneath the ground. The treasure consisted of 2,921 pounds of gold and 5,100 pounds of silver, as well as jewels obtained in St. Louis to help with transportation.

It is claimed that Beale placed the ciphers in a box, and left them with innkeeper, Robert Morriss, in Virginia in 1822 near where the treasure is said to have been buried. Beale promised to mail Morriss the keys, but apparently died before he could do so, and the keys were never received.

Eventually, 23 years later, Morriss's curiosity got the better of him and, assuming that Beale were dead, cracked open the locked box. Inside he found a note written by Beale in plain English and three sheets full of numbers.

Morriss unsuccessfully attempted to solve the ciphers on his own, but, decades later, ended up passing them to one of his friends. Using a particular edition of the American Declaration of Independence as the key, the friend successfully deciphered the second cipher, which gave descriptions of the buried treasure.

The friend ultimately made the ciphers public and wrote a pamphlet containing all three entitled The Beale Papers. He does not explain what led him to his solution of the second cipher text. There has been considerable debate over whether the remaining two ciphers are real or hoaxes.

So far, even the most skilled cryptanalysts who have attempted them have been defeated.

Most experts agree that the first and third ciphers have not been satisfactorily decoded.

The second Beale cipher, like the other two, contains about 800 numbers, beginning with the sequence; 115, 73, 24, 807, 37, ...

Beale's friend guessed that each number corresponded to a word in the Declaration of Independence. For example, the first number in the sequence is 115 – the 115th word of the Declaration is 'instituted', which begins with the letter "I". Hence the first number, 115, represents the letter 'I'. The second number in the sequence is 73 – the 73rd word in the Declaration is 'hold', thus an 'h' is the second letter of the decoded text.

THE BEGINNING OF THE "DECLARATION OF INDEPENDENCE"

When[1], in[2] the[3] course[4] of[5] human events it becomes
necessary[10] for one people to dissolve the political bands
which have[20] connected them with another, and to assume
among the powers[30] of the earth, the separate and equal
station to which[40] the laws of nature and of nature's God
entitle them[50], a decent respect to the opinions of mankind
requires that[60] they should declare the causes which impel
them to the[70] separation. We hold these truths to be self-evident,
and that[80] all men are created equal, that they are endowed
by[90] their Creator with certain inalienable rights, that among
these are[100] life, liberty and the pursuit of happiness; That
to secure[110] these rights, governments are instituted among men...

Cipher 1 - Location of the Vault

71,194,38,1701,89,76,11,83,1629,48,94,63,132,16,111,95,84,341

975,14,40,64,27,81,139,213,63,90,1120,8,15,3,126,2018,40,74

758,485,604,230,436,664,582,150,251,284,308,231,124,211,486,225

401,370,11,101,305,139,189,17,33,88,208,193,145,1,94,73,416

918,263,28,500,538,356,117,136,219,27,176,130,10,460,25,485,18

436,65,84,200,283,118,320,138,36,416,280,15,71,224,961,44,16,401

39,88,61,304,12,21,24,283,134,92,63,246,486,682,7,219,184,360,780

18,64,463,474,131,160,79,73,440,95,18,64,581,34,69,128,367,460,17

81,12,103,820,62,110,97,103,862,70,60,1317,471,540,208,121,890

346,36,150,59,568,614,13,120,63,219,812,2160,1780,99,35,18,21,136

872,15,28,170,88,4,30,44,112,18,147,436,195,320,37,122,113,6,140

8,120,305,42,58,461,44,106,301,13,408,680,93,86,116,530,82,568,9

102,38,416,89,71,216,728,965,818,2,38,121,195,14,326,148,234,18

55,131,234,361,824,5,81,623,48,961,19,26,33,10,1101,365,92,88,181

275,346,201,206,86,36,219,324,829,840,64,326,19,48,122,85,216,284

919,861,326,985,233,64,68,232,431,960,50,29,81,216,321,603,14,612

81,360,36,51,62,194,78,60,200,314,676,112,4,28,18,61,136,247,819

921,1060,464,895,10,6,66,119,38,41,49,602,423,962,302,294,875,78

14,23,111,109,62,31,501,823,216,280,34,24,150,1000,162,286,19,21

17,340,19,242,31,86,234,140,607,115,33,191,67,104,86,52,88,16,80

121,67,95,122,216,548,96,11,201,77,364,218,65,667,890,236,154,211

10,98,34,119,56,216,119,71,218,1164,1496,1817,51,39,210,36,3,19

540,232,22,141,617,84,290,80,46,207,411,150,29,38,46,172,85,194

39,261,543,897,624,18,212,416,127,931,19,4,63,96,12,101,418,16,140

230,460,538,19,27,88,612,1431,90,716,275,74,83,11,426,89,72,84

1300,1706,814,221,132,40,102,34,868,975,1101,84,16,79,23,16,81,122

324,403,912,227,936,447,55,86,34,43,212,107,96,314,264,1065,323

428,601,203,124,95,216,814,2906,654,820,2,301,112,176,213,71,87,96

202,35,10,2,41,17,84,221,736,820,214,11,60,760

Cipher 2 (not titled)

115,73,24,807,37,52,49,17,31,62,647,22,7,15,140,47,29,107,79,84

56,239,10,26,811,5,196,308,85,52,160,136,59,211,36,9,46,316,554

122,106,95,53,58,2,42,7,35,122,53,31,82,77,250,196,56,96,118,71

140,287,28,353,37,1005,65,147,807,24,3,8,12,47,43,59,807,45,316

101,41,78,154,1005,122,138,191,16,77,49,102,57,72,34,73,85,35,371

59,196,81,92,191,106,273,60,394,620,270,220,106,388,287,63,3,6

191,122,43,234,400,106,290,314,47,48,81,96,26,115,92,158,191,110

77,85,197,46,10,113,140,353,48,120,106,2,607,61,420,811,29,125,14

20,37,105,28,248,16,159,7,35,19,301,125,110,486,287,98,117,511,62

51,220,37,113,140,807,138,540,8,44,287,388,117,18,79,344,34,20,59

511,548,107,603,220,7,66,154,41,20,50,6,575,122,154,248,110,61,52,33

30,5,38,8,14,84,57,540,217,115,71,29,84,63,43,131,29,138,47,73,239

540,52,53,79,118,51,44,63,196,12,239,112,3,49,79,353,105,56,371,557

211,505,125,360,133,143,101,15,284,540,252,14,205,140,344,26,811,138

115,48,73,34,205,316,607,63,220,7,52,150,44,52,16,40,37,158,807,37

121,12,95,10,15,35,12,131,62,115,102,807,49,53,135,138,30,31,62,67,41

85,63,10,106,807,138,8,113,20,32,33,37,353,287,140,47,85,50,37,49,47

64,6,7,71,33,4,43,47,63,1,27,600,208,230,15,191,246,85,94,511,2,270

20,39,7,33,44,22,40,7,10,3,811,106,44,486,230,353,211,200,31,10,38

140,297,61,603,320,302,666,287,2,44,33,32,511,548,10,6,250,557,246

53,37,52,83,47,320,38,33,807,7,44,30,31,250,10,15,35,106,160,113,31

102,406,230,540,320,29,66,33,101,807,138,301,316,353,320,220,37,52

28,540,320,33,8,48,107,50,811,7,2,113,73,16,125,11,110,67,102,807,33

59,81,158,38,43,581,138,19,85,400,38,43,77,14,27,8,47,138,63,140,44

35,22,177,106,250,314,217,2,10,7,1005,4,20,25,44,48,7,26,46,110,230

807,191,34,112,147,44,110,121,125,96,41,51,50,140,56,47,152,540

63,807,28,42,250,138,582,98,643,32,107,140,112,26,85,138,540,53,20

125,371,38,36,10,52,118,136,102,420,150,112,71,14,20,7,24,18,12,807

37,67,110,62,33,21,95,220,511,102,811,30,83,84,305,620,15,2,108,220

106,353,105,106,60,275,72,8,50,205,185,112,125,540,65,106,807,188,96,110

16,73,32,807,150,409,400,50,154,285,96,106,316,270,205,101,811,400,8

44,37,52,40,241,34,205,38,16,46,47,85,24,44,15,64,73,138,807,85,78,110

33,420,505,53,37,38,22,31,10,110,106,101,140,15,38,3,5,44,7,98,287

135,150,96,33,84,125,807,191,96,511,118,440,370,643,466,106,41,107

603,220,275,30,150,105,49,53,287,250,208,134,7,53,12,47,85,63,138,110

21,112,140,485,486,505,14,73,84,575,1005,150,200,16,42,5,4,25,42

8,16,811,125,160,32,205,603,807,81,96,405,41,600,136,14,20,28,26

353,302,246,8,131,160,140,84,440,42,16,811,40,67,101,102,194,138

205,51,63,241,540,122,8,10,63,140,47,48,140,288

CIPHER 2 DECODED

I have deposited in the county of Bedford about four miles from Bufords (sic) in an excavation or vault six feet below the surface of the ground the following articles belonging jointly to the parties whose names are given in number three herewith. The first deposit consisted of ten hundred and fourteen pounds of gold and thirty eight hundred and twelve pounds of silver deposited Nov eighteen nineteen. The second was made Dec eighteen twenty one and consisted of nineteen hundred and seven pounds of gold and twelve hundred and eighty eight of silver, also jewels obtained in St. Louis in exchange to save transportation and valued at thirteen [t]housand dollars. The above is securely packed i[n] [i]ron pots with iron cov[e]rs. Th[e] vault is roughly lined with stone and the vessels rest on solid stone and are covered [w]ith others. Paper number one describes th[e] exact locality of the va[u]lt so that no difficulty will be had in finding it.

Cipher 3 - Names and Residences

317,8,92,73,112,89,67,318,28,96,107,41,631,78,146,397,118,98

114,246,348,116,74,88,12,65,32,14,81,19,76,121,216,85,33,66,15

108,68,77,43,24,122,96,117,36,211,301,15,44,11,46,89,18,136,68

317,28,90,82,304,71,43,221,198,176,310,319,81,99,264,380,56,37

319,2,44,53,28,44,75,98,102,37,85,107,117,64,88,136,48,154,99,175

89,315,326,78,96,214,218,311,43,89,51,90,75,128,96,33,28,103,84

65,26,41,246,84,270,98,116,32,59,74,66,69,240,15,8,121,20,77,80

31,11,106,81,191,224,328,18,75,52,82,117,201,39,23,217,27,21,84

35,54,109,128,49,77,88,1,81,217,64,55,83,116,251,269,311,96,54,32

120,18,132,102,219,211,84,150,219,275,312,64,10,106,87,75,47,21

29,37,81,44,18,126,115,132,160,181,203,76,81,299,314,337,351,96,11

28,97,318,238,106,24,93,3,19,17,26,60,73,88,14,126,138,234,286

297,321,365,264,19,22,84,56,107,98,123,111,214,136,7,33,45,40,13

28,46,42,107,196,227,344,198,203,247,116,19,8,212,230,31,6,328

65,48,52,59,41,122,33,117,11,18,25,71,36,45,83,76,89,92,31,65,70

83,96,27,33,44,50,61,24,112,136,149,176,180,194,143,171,205,296

87,12,44,51,89,98,34,41,208,173,66,9,35,16,95,8,113,175,90,56

203,19,177,183,206,157,200,218,260,291,305,618,951,320,18,124,78

65,19,32,124,48,53,57,84,96,207,244,66,82,119,71,11,86,77,213,54

82,316,245,303,86,97,106,212,18,37,15,81,89,16,7,81,39,96,14,43

216,118,29,55,109,136,172,213,64,8,227,304,611,221,364,819,375

128,296,1,18,53,76,10,15,23,19,71,84,120,134,66,73,89,96,230,48

77,26,101,127,936,218,439,178,171,61,226,313,215,102,18,167,262

114,218,66,59,48,27,19,13,82,48,162,119,34,127,139,34,128,129,74

63,120,11,54,61,73,92,180,66,75,101,124,265,89,96,126,274,896,917

434,461,235,890,312,413,328,381,96,105,217,66,118,22,77,64,42,12

7,55,24,83,67,97,109,121,135,181,203,219,228,256,21,34,77,319,374

382,675,684,717,864,203,4,18,92,16,63,82,22,46,55,69,74,112,134

186,175,119,213,416,312,343,264,119,186,218,343,417,845,951,124

209,49,617,856,924,936,72,19,28,11,35,42,40,66,85,94,112,65,82

115,119,233,244,186,172,112,85,6,56,38,44,85,72,32,47,63,96,124

217,314,319,221,644,817,821,934,922,416,975,10,22,18,46,137,181

101,39,86,103,116,138,164,212,218,296,815,380,412,460,495,675,820 952

Anyone tempted to take up the challenge of the Beale ciphers should heed the words of caution given by the author of the pamphlet:

"Before giving the papers to the public, I would give them a little advice, acquired by bitter experience. It is, to devote only such time as can be spared from your legitimate business to the task, and if you can spare no time, let the matter alone... Never, as I have done, sacrifice your own and your family's interests to what may prove an illusion; but, as I have already said, when your day's work is done, and you are comfortably seated by your good fire, a short time devoted to the subject can injure no one, and may bring its reward."

BEALE CIPHER SOLVED?

Has the Beale Cipher finally been solved? Yes, according to a Steven Ninichuck a retired electronics technician from Ohio and former military serviceman. Steven recently reports that he and Daniel Cole, a puzzle solver, a Mason of very high degree, and recipient of the Bronze Star in the Korean War have deciphered the documents from a Masonic ritual along with Gary Hutchinson, a local businessman. Tantalizingly, however, Steven has not shown how the ciphers were decoded but he does show photographs of what he claims are the vault along with the deciphered 'location' cipher.

Steven says, "Upon our locating the Excavation Site we quickly discovered the vault was no longer intact. Evidence at the site indicated that someone had located the vault long ago and that the contents are long gone. So far only a few items have been discovered during our excavations, these items were all discovered at the upper vault entrance. A more extensive excavation of the surrounding area is planned this year and hopefully the snake and hornet encounters will not hamper our efforts as they have in the past!"

The Location Cipher

According to Dan Cole, the Location Cipher deciphers as:

Nineteen is the distance south, Left onto
second point. Two's on first part of main
rock south in east wall, Ground on souths
six feet deep. Open front side of point
straight down the point in front upper part.
Remove rocks, Then with them remove dirt
five feet down and round. On Now, Open point
two's wall straight in, Now open south side,
Now On down under point.

As further proof that someone was previously at the vault, Steve
shows a belt buckle that he found while excavating the vault entrance.

24

LETTER FROM GARY HUTCHINSON

Audrey and I first met Daniel Cole in the early summer of 1999 at our antique store in Bethel, Ohio. We took an instant liking to him and him to us. Dan had a Masonic background so he and I had a common bond. After a time we grew to trust one another and what we said and how we acted was as masons always put it, "on the square".

Dan began by telling us of an immense treasure that he knew of and was positive of its location. Both my wife and I never heard of the Beale treasure or the legend that surrounded it. He claimed to have documents and other information that confirmed its location. Dan had offered this general information to few people and then only to family and a few trusted friends. We decided that what he had told us was well worth investigating.

We met at Dan's home one evening and he began to explain in great detail the information concerning his findings.

Dan explained the ciphers and how they pointed to a particular area in Bedford County, Virginia. Dan had been compiling the history of the Beale treasure since 1990. He had a talent for working on codes; his background in the military during the Korean War was a great benefit in his understanding of codes and ciphers. There was no doubt in his mind that the legend of Thomas Beale was based on fact and not fiction. The reason for the treasures existence was directly tied to the Thomas Jefferson era and the fragile political existence of the United States at that time.

We listened to Dan for many hours and asked him questions that were all answered to our satisfaction. He was absolutely sure that the Beale treasure did exist and that the ciphers were not part of an elaborate hoax. Audrey and I were convinced with Dan's work and agreed to participate in the search.

Dan told us where the cipher had led him and that the cipher was not entirely completed, but he knew the treasure was deposited on a small farm nestled in the Blue Ridge Mountains not far from the old settlement of Bufford (sic), which presently is known as Montvale, Virginia. In order to proceed further with our search we needed permission to access to the property. Some years ago the land owner had approved but now had a change of heart and refused access. A woman named Mary Given owned the farm at that time. Dan told us that the farm or portions of it were for sale. He thought that one of the lots containing the location of the treasure could be purchased, however, Audrey and I thought that it would be to everyone's benefit to buy the whole farm. We purchased the property on February 7, 2000 and gained access one month later.

The property had been a focal point for many in the search for the Beale treasure. For instance, one man by the name of G.W. Hunt had been given permission by the land owner "Mrs. Given" to live on the farm and search for the treasure. He did so for nearly some twenty years until his demise.

Mr. Hunt died on the farm some years ago possibly not realizing just how close he actually was to the treasure vault. His interpretation of the cipher must have been very close but it would seem he used a wrong formation of rock on Goose Creek.

Evidence of his digging still exists on a foothill of Porters Mountain just south of Goose Creek. We mistakenly used the same formation as our starting point too; this led us to digging in several spots along the creek during the summer of 2000. Each spot chosen for excavation fit many points in the cipher but there just wasn't enough correlation to make it exactly right.

Dan continued to check his work and refine the cipher until his death early February of 2001. The third member of our party, Steve Ninichuck, had made the observation that a certain rock formation just off [the] road held a high interest to him. This particular formation seemed to have been partially destroyed when a new road was constructed some 50 years ago. One can only imagine how large and pronounced this point was with its cliff like features before the road was cut around it. Our search had been failing using other reference points but finally at last we now had the completed cipher directions that Dan had finished for us. We began at the first and now smaller rock formation. During the first week of June 2001, Steve and I began clearing brush and excavating an area over the cliff face.

We were using '19' as the distance south from this point. The cipher did not tell us what form of measurement to use, so we wondered if it meant nineteen feet or nineteen yards. Neither distance seemed to put us in a place as described by the cipher so we decided the only other measurement had to be in rods; this was a more commonly used distance measurement of that time period.

We began by clearing a path due south across the cliff top of the first point so we could measure the distance accurately. The measurement of nineteen rods starts directly from across the creek where the east water begins and leads directly over the first point and down a small ravine to a rock formation containing an east wall. This area contained a small cave with a rocky point and an underlying ledge.

Steve had found this location on a previous search while Dan was still with us. None of the directions we knew at that time could prove that the small cave was the actual vault used by Beale. Still unconvinced with our find, we continued with our search. Meanwhile Dan continued his work at home and continued to look the cipher over carefully. Later it was to our surprise that Dan had been correct all along with his decoding of the cipher. Our only problem with the reading of the cipher came from various "short" words. Some of these words were misinterpreted in the lower portion of the cipher and prevented us from finding the proper landmarks required to locate the vault.

The rock cave had obviously been eroded over the years and one could see that the little cave had been somewhat larger years ago.

Our final conclusion is that the proper measurement had been taken and indeed it did lead us to the only place where the treasure could have been hidden. Our excavation of the site provided evidence that it had been used, an iron leg from a pot was found with a few other items. Needless to say we are extremely disappointed with the outcome of our adventure, the directions are too precise to lead elsewhere and with that we end our search.

In closing I wish to quote a few words from Thomas Jefferson Beale: "keep on perservering, the rewards awaiting you are so vast you will find it hard to comprehend."

What's next for the Beale Treasure?

Have Steven Ninichuck and his team finally solved one of the greatest treasure hunts of all time? What became of the Beale treasure? Why didn't Beale and his fellow adventurers return to claim their treasure? When will we see how the Location cipher was broken?
We shall have to wait for further evidence.

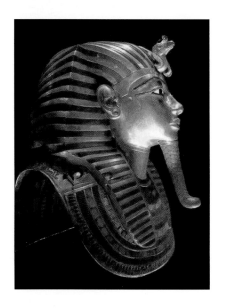

Tutankhamen, the boy king, ruled Egypt in the eighteenth dynasty after he was given the throne at the age of eight; yet, he ruled only briefly until his unexpected death. The treasure in King Tutankhamen's tomb was untouched until 1922 when Howard Carter and Lord Carnarvon uncovered the tomb beneath the mud brick houses of the workmen who cut the tomb of Ramesses VI. Most likely, this tomb was not made for a king, but rather for a high official. The tomb was probably used because a suitable pyramid had not been built for the boy king, thus the rooms were hastily prepared with the items for his afterlife seemingly thrown into the various rooms.

Over 3,000 treasures were placed in the tomb to help Tutankhamen in his afterlife and the walls of the burial chamber were painted with scenes of his voyage to the afterworld. The burial chamber contained four gilded shrines; inside was a red quartzite sarcophagus containing three nested coffins. Tutankhamen's mummy rested in a coffin made of solid gold. His body was wrapped in linen and over his face was placed an exquisite gold mask.

The Curse of the Mummy

On April 5, 1923, soon after opening King Tutankhamen's tomb, Lord Carnarvon became seriously ill from an infected mosquito bite. During his illness he spoke the name of Tutankhamen several times. A doctor, sent to examine him, arrived too late and Lord Carnarvon died. Reportedly, at that moment, the lights in Cairo mysteriously went out.

The inscription contained on the tomb's seal had become reality:

"He who disturbs the pharaoh's sleep shall be touched by the wings of death."

A couple of weeks later, Colonel Audrey Herbert, the youngest brother of Lord Carnarvon also died suddenly, followed shortly by the nurse that cared for him. Next, Carter's private secretary died. His father, who was conducting a study of the objects in the royal tomb, was next. Then, Mace, one of Carter's co-work-

ers died. In two years, 17 scholars associated with opening King Tutankhamen's tomb would die.

It is also claimed that a cobra killed Howard Carter's pet canary after the discovery of King Tutankhamen's tomb. And it is reported that

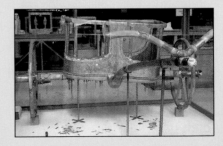

Lord Carnarvon's dog howled and dropped dead at two in the morning when Carnarvon died.

Did King Tutankhamen's Tomb really unleash a curse? Perhaps, but Howard Carter lived a decade after his major discovery. Today, King Tutankhamen's treasures can be found in the Cairo Museum.

KHUFU'S GREAT PYRAMID

The 'Great Pyramid' of Khufu was the tallest building in the world until the 19th century and, at 4,500 years old, is the only one of the famous Seven Wonders of the Ancient World that still stands.

Khufu, like all the dead pharaohs of his time, was probably buried with the things that he would need in the after-life as many pharaohs were buried with untold treasures.

To protect the pharaoh's treasures from tomb robbers, Egyptian architects often designed pyramids with secret passageways that could be plugged with impassable granite blocks, created secret rooms, and made decoy chambers.

In 820 A.D., Caliph Abdullah Al Manum discovered a secret hinged door in Khufu's pyramid that led into a passageway. The passageway descended to a blank wall. From there, an empty pit extended downward for 30 feet. Manun's workers also cut through several granite blocks to discover a horizontal passage that led to the empty 'Queen's chamber'. Above the chamber, they found a tall ascending passageway, now called the Grand Gallery. At the top of the gallery was a low horizontal passage that led to the 'King's Chamber'. In the center of the chamber was a large, empty granite sarcophagus without a lid. Otherwise the room was empty.

Extensive explorations have found no other chambers or passageways.

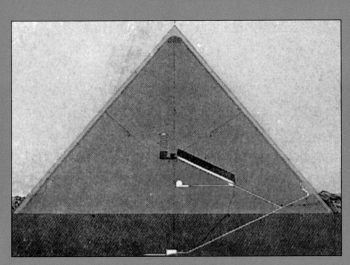

Diagram of the passages discovered
by Caliph Abdullah Al Manum

Modern workers in
the Grand Gallery

Where is the treasure of King Khufu? Was the pyramid the victim of robbers in ancient times? How could thieves get out with all of Khufu's treasure when the passages were still sealed? Where is Khufu's mummy? Did Khufu and his architects out smart both the ancient thieves and modern archaeologists? Are there yet undiscovered secret passages in Khufu's Great Pyramid that contain his vast treasure?

Nobody knows.

31

The Great Sphinx is located in Egypt on the Giza plateau about six miles west of Cairo. It was carved from a natural outcropping of rock around 2500 B.C. But, by the 19th century, when European archaeologists investigated the statue, it was covered up to its neck in sand.

The Sphinx, originally carved with the head of a woman, the body of a lion and the wings of a bird, was later re-carved in the likeness of a pharaoh.

Is The Sphinx Older Than We Think?

Most archaeologists believe that the Sphinx was carved during the reign of King Khafre around 2500 B.C. However, in 1979, John Anthony West, an amateur archaeologist, suggested that the Sphinx was far older than the pyramids and its severe erosion was the result of rain, not blowing sand. He concluded that the Sphinx must have been built thousands of years earlier when Egypt had much more rain.

Robert Schoch, a geologist from Boston University, later examined the Sphinx and also concluded that the erosions in the Sphinx were created by running water. He believed that the front and side of the Sphinx date from 5000 to 7000 B.C. and was remodeled during Khafre's era to give the likeness of the pharaoh. Other Egyptologists believe that the fissures found by Schoch were the result of wet sand being blown up from the Nile River, not rain.

In the 1940's, the American psychic Edgar Cayce predicted that a chamber would be found under the front paws of the Sphinx which would contain a library of records written by the survivors of Atlantis.

In 1995, workers renovating a parking lot near the Sphinx uncovered a series of empty tunnels and pathways, two of which go underground near the Sphinx.

Later, while examining the Sphinx for erosion, archaeologists using a seismograph found evidence of hollow, regularly shaped chambers a few meters below ground between the paws and to either side of the Sphinx.

To date, no further examination has been allowed.

Could the Sphinx be the result of a civilization 5000 years older than the Egyptians?

Does the Sphinx conceal secret chambers filled with treasure from Atlantis?

THE VOYNICH MANUSCRIPT

The Voynich Manuscript is considered by some to be the most mysterious manuscript in the world. To this day this medieval artifact resists all efforts at translation. It is either an ingenious hoax or an unbreakable cipher.

The manuscript is named after its discoverer, the American antique book dealer and collector, Wilfrid M. Voynich, who discovered it in 1912, among a collection of ancient manuscripts kept in villa Mondragone in Frascati, near Rome. The ancient text has no known title, no known author, and is written in no known language.

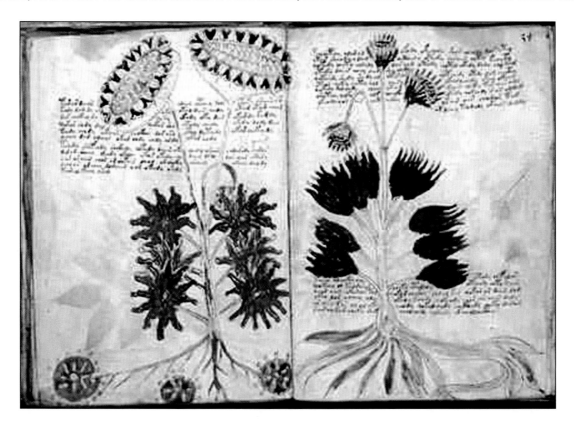

 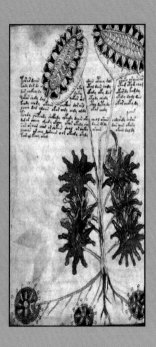  

The mysterious book was once bought by an emperor, forgotten on a library shelf, sold for thousands of dollars, and later donated to Yale.

One of the illustrations in the book appears to be somehow related to the Sun. The book also shows parts of the sky with unfamiliar constellations. Parts of the book appear to be about alchemy.

The Voynich Manuscript is about 6 by 9 inches. It contains the equivalent of 246 quarto pages. There are 212 pages with text and drawings, 33 pages contain text only. The text is written in an enciphered script, and the drawings are colored in red, blue, brown, yellow, and green.

The book remains in Yale University's rare book collection under catalog number MS 408.

Going up the Missouri River in 1856, on a trip to Kansas City and points north, the side-wheel steamer, Arabia, struck a walnut tree below the water and sank near Parkville, Missouri. Her 222 tons of frontier cargo and the possessions of the passengers disappeared below the silt of the river bottom and remained undisturbed until 1988. Fortunately, all of her crew and passengers were saved.

In 1987, local resident, Bob Hawley, his sons David and Greg and friend Jerry Mackey were looking for adventure. With the permission of the landowner, David began the search for the Arabia using old river maps and a metal detector. Within two hours, David Hawley found the wreck over a half mile from the meandering river's edge and 45 feet underground.

Eighteen months later, on November 13th 1988, Bob and his team returned and raised the Arabia.

The Arabia lay in an old underground river channel and before excavating it, the team had to pump out 20,000 gallons of water-per-minute back into the Missouri River, over a half mile away. For the next several months, the team recovered everything from crates of frontier merchandise including castor oil and cognac to needles and nutmegs. Also, raised from the Arabia were

DAVID HAWLEY, DISCOVERER OF THE SIDE-WHEELER ARABIA

Bob and Greg Hawley unloading a crate filled with French Cognac.

window panes, wedding bands, eyeglasses, earrings, underwear and umbrellas. Carpenter's tools, porcelain figurines, patched trousers and children's marbles were also found among the passenger's belongings.

Almost every box from the Arabia was different and included four thousand boots and shoes, ten thousand calico buttons and millions of glass beads. Finally, after removing all of the cargo, heavy equipment hoisted the 25,000 pound boiler, paddle wheel, and the stern.

THE ARABIA TREASURE TODAY

Did the members of the newly formed River Salvage Company sell their booty and collect a fortune? No. They cleaned, cataloged and placed the Arabia's treasures into a museum.

Today, the recovered parts of the Arabia, along with the entire contents of the sunken ship are housed in the Arabia Steamboat Museum in Kansas City, Missouri.

OTHER STEAMBOAT TREASURES

It was not uncommon for Steamboats to sink during the time of the Arabia. In 1897, historian H.M. Chittendon listed over 200 similar boats lost on the Missouri River between St. Louis and Kansas City.

9 SECRET CODE

PHAISTOS DISK

In 1903 the Phaistos Disk, one of the most puzzling objects ever discovered, was found in the Minoan palace at Hagia Triada on the Greek island of Crete.

The Disk is inscribed on both sides with a hieroglyphic text, arranged in bands, spiraling from the center. There are 241 figures including standing or running men, women, and children, heads with feather crowns, fish, birds, insects, vessels, shields, boughs, ships, tools, parts of animals, and others.

The inscription has never been deciphered.

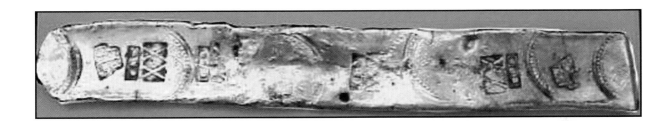

The Atocha, a Spanish treasure ship, sank in a storm somewhere in the Florida Keys in 1622 just two days after leaving port in Havana. Down with the ship went a fortune in silver and gold bars, emeralds, jewelry and hundreds of thousands of coins.

Built in 1620 in a Havana shipyard, the Atocha was designed as a guard galleon for the treasure fleets traveling between Spain and The New World. Her modern accommodations and the security of her armament made her the choice of nobility, government officials and wealthy merchants. With the addition of the passengers' own gold, silver, jewels and personal belongings to the Atocha's hull filled with treasures of the New World, the total value of treasure aboard reached astounding levels.

Two days out of Havana, the Atocha and her fleet were caught in a violent storm. Her foremast was gone and her sails tattered. Her stern caught in the wind, was lifted high on a wave, and smashed violently down onto a reef, ripping great holes in her hull. Most of those aboard were below decks, with the hatches securely fastened. Unable to escape in time, 260 crew and passengers were carried down when the ship quickly sank. Only five men lashed to the rigging survived.

Spain searched the ship for 70 years before finally giving up and it was not until 1985 that the treasure of the Atocha was found by Mel Fisher and a team of treasure hunters.

To date, items valued at hundreds of millions of dollars have been recovered including tons of silver and gold ingots from Potosi, emeralds from Columbia, copper from Cuba, and numerous rare Spanish artifacts.

The bulk of the treasure consisted of almost 47 tons of silver, over 150,000 gold coins and millions of dollars in precious gems.

Funded by the rich Atocha treasure, the company formed by Mel Fisher continues to search for treasure around the world.

The pirate Blackbeard was born Edward Teach of Bristol, England in 1680. He served on a privateer commissioned by Queen Anne to attack French and Spanish ships during the war of Spanish Succession, keeping what cargoes they captured. In 1691, he and his crew were supposed to have buried a large treasure of silver bars at Lunging Island off Portsmouth, New Hampshire, which has never been found.

Certainly Captain Kidd is one of the most famous of all the pirates, though he claimed up until the end that he wasn't a pirate.

Born William Kidd in 1645 in Grenock, Scotland, little is known of his early life other than he went to sea as a young boy. He served on a privateer against the French in the West Indies and North America and by 1690 he was a well known and wealthy merchant ship captain.

In London in 1695, Kidd received a royal commission to hunt pirates attacking East India Company ships in the Red Sea and Indian Ocean and was given the ship, Adventure Galley.

Captain Kidd did poorly against the pirates, and finally gave up and turned to piracy. In 1698 he was arrested for piracy and sent to England for trial.

Though he swore his innocence, he was found guilty of five counts of piracy and sentenced to be hanged. On May 23, 1701, the rope broke on the first attempt to carry out the sentence and he was hung a second time. His body was then tarred, wrapped in chains, and hung in an iron cage over the water at Tilbury Point for almost 20 years as a warning to other seamen.

Some of his treasure was recovered on Gardiner's Island off Long Island and the proceeds from the sale were given to charity.

The Kryptos sculpture sits on the grounds of the CIA Headquarters in Langley, Virginia. Its thousands of characters contain encrypted messages, of which three sections have been solved. The fourth section at the bottom remains unsolved, and is one of the most famous unsolved codes in the world.

The most famous part of the Kryptos puzzle is a wavy copper screen covered with about 1800 encrypted characters. It stands next to a petrified tree, a circular pool and several rocks. Other parts of the puzzle include several large slabs of granite with sheets of copper with Morse code messages and an engraved compass with a needle pointing at a lodestone.

The left side of the copper screen, the first two sections, is a table for deciphering and enciphering code, a method developed by 16th century French cryptographer Blaise de Vigenere.

James Sanborn, the designer of the sculpture, said "They will be able to read what I wrote, but what I wrote is a mystery itself."

Only time will tell if the final message to this puzzle is solved. If you want to try to break the code, here are the letters from "Kryptos."

The Kryptos Code   Left Side

```
E M U F P H Z L R F A X Y U S D J K Z L D K R N S H G N F I V J
Y Q T Q U X Q B Q V Y U V L L T R E V J Y Q T M K Y R D M F D
V F P J U D E E H Z W E T Z Y V G W H K K Q E T G F Q J N C E
G G W H K K ? D Q M C P F Q Z D Q M M I A G P F X H Q R L G
T I M V M Z J A N Q L V K Q E D A G D V F R P J U N G E U N A
Q Z G Z L E C G Y U X U E E N J T B J L B Q C R T B J D F H R R
Y I Z E T K Z E M V D U F K S J H K F W H K U W Q L S Z F T I
H H D D D U V H ? D W K B F U F P W N T D F I Y C U Q Z E R E
E V L D K F E Z M O Q Q J L T T U G S Y Q P F E U N L A V I D X
F L G G T E Z ? F K Z B S F D Q V G O G I P U F X H H D R K F
F H Q N T G P U A E C N U V P D J M Q C L Q U M U N E D F Q
E L Z Z V R R G K F F V O E E X B D M V P N F Q X E Z L G R E
D N Q F M P N Z G L F L P M R J Q Y A L M G N U V P D X V K P
D Q U M E B E D M H D A F M J G Z N U P L G E W J L L A E T G
E N D Y A H R O H N L S R H E O C P T E O I B I D Y S H N A I A
C H T N R E Y U L D S L L S L L N O H S N O S M R W X M N E
T P R N G A T I H N R A R P E S L N N E L E B L P I I A C A E
W M T W N D I T E E N R A H C T E N E U D R E T N H A E O E
T F O L S E D T I W E N H A E I O Y T E Y Q H E E N C T A Y C R
E I F T B R S P A M H N E W E N A T A M A T E G Y E E R L B
T E E F O A S F I O T U E T U A E O T O A R M A E E R T N R T I
B S E D D N I A A H T T M S T E W P I E R O A G R I E W F E B
A E C T D D H I L C E I H S I T E G O E A O S D D R Y D L O R I T
gR K L M L E H A G T D H A R D P N E O H M G F M F E U H E
E C D M R I P F E I M E H N L S S T T R T V D O H W ? O B K R
U O X O G H U L B S O L I F B B W F L R V Q Q P R N G K S S O
T W T Q S J Q S S E K Z Z W A T J K L U D I A W I N F B N Y P
V T T M Z F P K W G D K Z X T J C D I G K U H U A U E K C A R
```

```
  A B C D E F G H I J K L M N O P Q R S T U V W X Y Z A B C D
A K R Y P T O S A B C D E F G H I J L M N Q U V W X Z K R Y P
B R Y P T O S A B C D E F G H I J L M N Q U V W X Z K R Y P T
C Y P T O S A B C D E F G H I J L M N Q U V W X Z K R Y P T O
D P T O S A B C D E F G H I J L M N Q U V W X Z K R Y P T O S
E T O S A B C D E F G H I J L M N Q U V W X Z K R Y P T O S A
F O S A B C D E F G H I J L M N Q U V W X Z K R Y P T O S A B
G S A B C D E F G H I J L M N Q U V W X Z K R Y P T O S A B C
H A B C D E F G H I J L M N Q U V W X Z K R Y P T O S A B C D
I B C D E F G H I J L M N Q U V W X Z K R Y P T O S A B C D E
J C D E F G H I J L M N Q U V W X Z K R Y P T O S A B C D E F
K D E F G H I J L M N Q U V W X Z K R Y P T O S A B C D E F G
L E F G H I J L M N Q U V W X Z K R Y P T O S A B C D E F G H
M F G H I J L M N Q U V W X Z K R Y P T O S A B C D E F G H I
N G H I J L M N Q U V W X Z K R Y P T O S A B C D E F G H I J
O H I J L M N Q U V W X Z K R Y P T O S A B C D E F G H I J L
P I J L M N Q U V W X Z K R Y P T O S A B C D E F G H I J L M
Q J L M N Q U V W X Z K R Y P T O S A B C D E F G H I J L M N
R L M N Q U V W X Z K R Y P T O S A B C D E F G H I J L M N Q
S M N Q U V W X Z K R Y P T O S A B C D E F G H I J L M N Q U
T N Q U V W X Z K R Y P T O S A B C D E F G H I J L M N Q U V
U Q U V W X Z K R Y P T O S A B C D E F G H I J L M N Q U V W
V U V W X Z K R Y P T O S A B C D E F G H I J L M N Q U V W X
W V W X Z K R Y P T O S A B C D E F G H I J L M N Q U V W X Z
X W X Z K R Y P T O S A B C D E F G H I J L M N Q U V W X Z K
Y X Z K R Y P T O S A B C D E F G H I J L M N Q U V W X Z K R
Z Z K R Y P T O S A B C D E F G H I J L M N Q U V W X Z K R Y
```

Armchair Treasure Hunting began in 1979 with Kit Williams' book Masquerade. Masquerade was written as a children's story and encouraged the reader to examine every picture in fine detail in order to locate the hidden clues to a buried "Golden Hare".

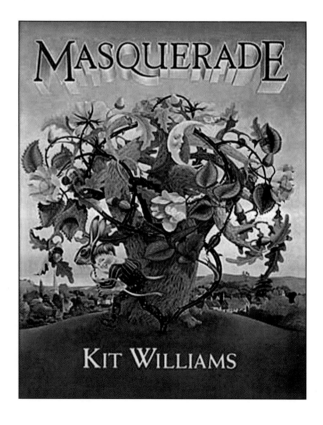

The treasure for Masquerade was an 18 carat gold hare made by Kit and adorned with precious stones. The hare had a value at the time of about £5000.

CIPHERS

14 CIPHERS

A cipher is a way of concealing the meaning of something written.

A simple 'transposition' cipher does not change any letters of the original message, but rather changes the position of the letters. A transposition cipher could reverse the order of the letters of each word. For example, the message 'Right before your eyes' becomes 'thgir erofeb ruoy seye'.

A slightly more complex cipher, the substitution cipher, keeps the order of the letters in the message, but changes them with other letters. Each letter of the message is replaced by another letter or symbol. For example, Morse code is a substitution cipher in which each letter is replaced by a specific set of dots and dashes.

A well-known substitution cipher is called a Shift Cipher or Caesar Cipher. In the Shift Cipher, the standard alphabet is shifted so that another letter in the alphabet is substituted for each letter as follows:

A	B	C	D	E	F	G	H	I	J	K	L	M	N	O	P	Q	R	S	T	U	V	W	X	Y	Z
G	H	I	J	K	L	M	N	O	P	Q	R	S	T	U	V	W	X	Y	Z	A	B	C	D	E	F

Using this cipher, the message 'RIGHT BEFORE YOUR EYES' becomes 'XOMNZ HKLUXK EUAX KEKY'.

Vigenere Ciphers

Blaise de Vigenere , a 16th century French diplomat, developed a simple and elegant cipher that was difficult to crack. A Vigenere cipher uses 26 substitution ciphers as shown below:

A BCD EFGH IJK LMNO PQR STUV WXYZ   A BCD EFGH IJK LMNO PQR STUV WXYZ

01: A BCD EFGH IJK LMNO PQR STUV WXYZ
02: B CDE FGHI JKL MNOP QRS TUVW XYZA
03: C DEF GHIJ KLM NOPQ RST UVWX YZAB
04: D EFG HIJK LMN OPQR STU VWXY ZABC
05: E FGH IJKL MNO PQRS TUV WXYZ ABCD
06: F GHI JKLM NOP QRST UVW XYZA BCDE
07: G HIJ KLMN OPQ RSTU VWX YZAB CDEF
08: H IJK LMNO PQR STUV WXY ZABC DEFG
09: I JKL MNOP QRS TUVW XYZ ABCD EFGH
10: J KLM NOPQ RST UVWX YZA BCDE FGHI
11: K LMN OPQR STU VWXY ZAB CDEF GHIJ
12: L MNO PQRS TUV WXYZ ABC DEFG HIJK
13: M NOP QRST UVW XYZA BCD EFGH IJKL

14: N OPQ RSTU VWX YZAB CDE FGHI JKLM
15: O PQR STUV WXY ZABC DEF GHIJ KLMN
16: P QRS TUVW XYZ ABCD EFG HIJK LMNO
17: Q RST UVWX YZA BCDE FGH IJKL MNOP
18: R STU VWXY ZAB CDEF GHI JKLM NOPQ
19: S TUV WXYZ ABC DEFG HIJ KLMN OPQR
20: T UVW XYZA BCD EFGH IJK LMNO PQRS
21: U VWX YZAB CDE FGHI JKL MNOP QRST
22: V WXY ZABC DEF GHIJ KLM NOPQ RSTU
23: W XYZ ABCD EFG HIJK LMN OPQR STUV
24: X YZA BCDE FGH IJKL MNO PQRS TUVW
25: Y ZAB CDEF GHI JKLM NOP QRST UVWX
26: Z ABC DEFG HIJ KLMN OPQ RSTU VWXY

The Vigenere cipher uses a 'key' to select different cipher alphabets in succession. The key can be any word or phrase such as 'TREASURE'.

For example, to encipher the phrase 'RIGHT BEFORE YOUR EYES' using the key word 'TREA-SURE', just scan down to the first 'T' and go over to the column headed with an 'R'. The first letter of the enciphered word would then be a 'K' (the intersection of the T and R – printed in red).

The whole message is enciphered, repeating this process as follows:

Keyword T and message R intersect at K

Keyword R and message I intersect at Z

Keyword E and message G intersect at K

Keyword A and message H intersect at H

Keyword S and message T intersect at L

Keyword U and message B intersect at V

Keyword R and message E intersect at V

Keyword E and message F intersect at J

Keyword T and message O intersect at H

Keyword R and message R intersect at I

Keyword E and message E intersect at I

Keyword A and message Y intersect at Y

Keyword S and message O intersect at G

Keyword U and message U intersect at O

Keyword R and message R intersect at I

Keyword E and message E intersect at I

Keyword T and message Y intersect at R

Keyword R and message E intersect at V

Keyword E and message S intersect at W

Thus, the message 'RIGHT BEFORE YOUR EYES' enciphers into 'KZKHL VVJHII YGOI IRVM'.

To decipher the message to its original meaning, start with the first letter of the keyword, 'T' and read across until you find the 'K' and read up to the top to get an 'R'. And so on to get the original phrase.

Ciphers also show up in Edgar Allen Poe's fictional short story, THE GOLD BUG, where the hero cracks the following cipher:

" 53‡‡†305))6*;4826)4‡.)4‡);806*;48†8¶60))85;1‡(;:‡*8†83(88)
5*†;46(;88*96*?;8)*‡(;485);5*†2:*‡(;4956*2(5*—4)8¶8*;40692
85);)6†8)4‡‡;1(‡9;48081;8:8‡1;48†85;4)485†528806*81(‡9;48;(8
8;4(‡?34;48)4‡;161;:188;‡?;"

as:

"A good glass in the bishop's hostel in the devil's seat—forty-one degrees and thirteen minutes—northeast and by north—main branch seventh limb east side—shoot from the left eye of the death's-head—a bee-line from the tree through the shot fifty feet out."

The message leads the hero to the buried treasure of the pirate Captain Kidd.

In the story, a substitution cipher is used to replace each character in the cipher with another based on the frequency of normal occurrence of letters in the English language. The story declares that e is the most frequently used letter with the rest of the letters occurring as follows: a o i d h n r s t u y c f g l m w b k p q x z. By counting the number of times each character appeared in the cipher, the hero deciphers the message.

Sherlock Holmes, the fictional detective created by Sir Arthur Conan Doyle, cracks a cipher based on stickman figures in The Adventure of the Dancing Men.

Holmes uses a similar analysis as in Poe's story and deciphers:

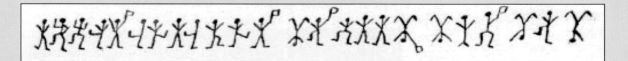

He declares, "If you use the code which I have explained you will find that it simply means 'Come here at once'."

French author, Jules Verne, also used cryptography in his novel Journey to the Center of The Earth, in which an ancient parchment is deciphered and tells the path to the Earth's interior.

PUZZLES &
ILLUSIONS

What is the next element in this series?

Still having trouble?

Well, what is the next element in this series?

Still having a problem?

Then, what's the next element in this series?

1 2 3 4 5 6 7

(Hint: All three of these series are related!)

Which is the largest state?

PIGPEN CIPHER

The pigpen cipher is called that because you draw little pigpens around the key. *Can you decipher the following code?*

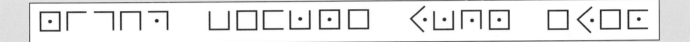

DUCK OR RABBIT?

Five boxes become four—right before your eyes! How did this happen?

1. Note the five red boxes.

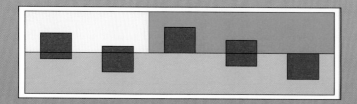

2. Separate the top half of the diagram.

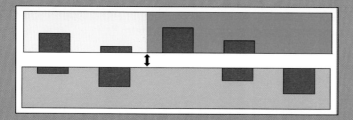

3. Cut the top into two pieces.

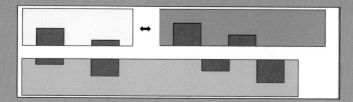

4. Exchange the left half and the right half.

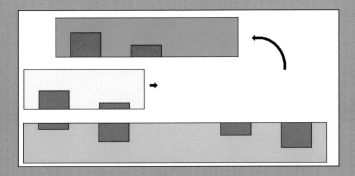

5. Move the top half back into place.

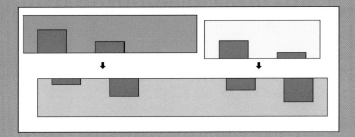

6. Presto! Four boxes. One box has vanished. How?

21 PUZZLE — CRYPTOQUOTE

GKKA'O LDEO ORKI JG. TDQ RDW VLLZ ILCCMZS IRL IEJIR! IELLO QKJCW IDCA!

22 PUZZLE — ILLUSION

Do you see a non-existent white triangle in the figure below?

23 PUZZLE — HIDDEN ANIMAL

Have you ever not been able to see the forest because of the trees? What animal is hiding in the following symbols?

24 PUZZLE

RIDDLE OF THE SPHINX
(THIS IS AN OLDIE, SO THINK ACCORDINGLY)

In Greek mythology, the sphinx guarded the gates of the city of Thebes and challenged all who entered with a riddle.

"What goes on four legs in the morning, on two legs at noon and on three legs at dusk?"

The sphinx killed all who could not answer the riddle and promised to destroy herself if anyone ever answered the riddle.

Oedipus solved the riddle? *Can you?*

25 PUZZLE

CRYPTOQUOTE

NOGGAL OL SNOW REED'W HEVGW CLG BOFSUVAW CVA SNA FPUAW SE SNA SHAPYA

QAHAPAG FVACSUVAW OL SNA WSEVT. OK TEU FCL KOLG SNA FPUAW CLG WEPYA

SNAZ —CLG OK TEU RAPOAYA OL KCOVOAW—OS HOPP RA TEUV WSEVT.

26 SOUND ILLUSION

ILLUSION

Count every F you see an in the following sentence:

Frenzied fairies fought off forty of the most fiendish fiends from the far side of the forest.

How many did you find?

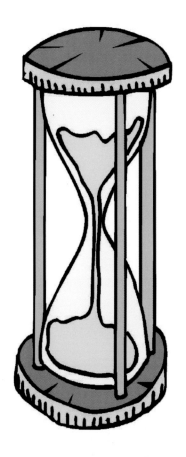

27 PUZZLE   *TRIANGLE PIECES?*

Can you assemble
the following shapes
to make a triangle?

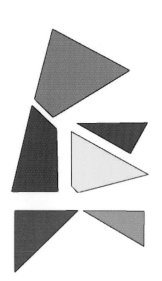

28 PUZZLE   *U.S. GEOGRAPHY*

Which state in the contiguous 48 states borders
the least number of states?

DECEPTIVE TRIANGLE

Are the sides of
the triangle bent
inward or are
they straight?

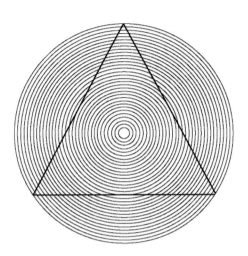

CRYPTOQUOTE

SAW TRRSWUESRRIZSE, FAR AND LWWU FNOUWD LY YRONA

URS SR DR NUYSAZUK NS NPP, ENS RU SAW BPRRO NUD

IPNYWD FZSA LZSE RB SAW NPHAWCZES'E SRRPE - HRIIWO

HRZPE, HROT ESRIIWOE NUD EAZUY KPNEE HRUSNZUWOE.

Based on the following Morse code table, a message could easily be hidden in a common picture..

A .- B -... C -.-. D -.. E . F ..-. G --. H .... I .. J .--- K -.- L .-.. M --
N -. O --- P .--. Q --.- R .-. S ... T - U ..- V ...- W .-- X -..- Y -.-- Z --..

PART 1: Form a new word from each of the following:

HEIGHT   FRINGE   POTIONS   RESCUE   SLIGHT   UNTIED   VOWELS

PART 2: Decode the following sentence using the anagrams above:

RESCUE POTIONS! HEIGHT FRINGE SLIGHT UNTIED VOWELS.

34

PUZZLE

CLASSIC RIDDLES

At night they come without being fetched,
And by day they are lost without being stolen.

35

PUZZLE

CRYPTOQUOTE

JO DEAR LIBSTRA ABDPKRT, J VKYZGRAYSM OIJVL EV OBSKYMIL OBTTRSKU XYRAZRT LIR

ZKEBTO JST OLABZG LIR QRWRKO, DJGYSM LIRD OXJAGKR JST MKYLLRA - JO YV NJZ IRKT J

IJSTVBK EV OLJAO.

Are the vertical lines in the following illustration crooked or straight?

Stare at the black
dot in the center of
the gray area.

After a few seconds
the gray area will
start to disappear.

38 PUZZLE *ILLUSION*

Is it possible to make the
following shape?

Can you assemble
the following shapes
to make a hexagon?

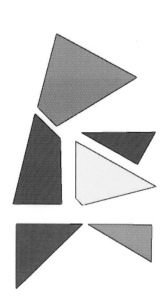

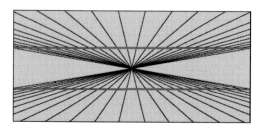

Are the two blue lines bent?

41 PUZZLE CRYPTOQUOTE

FJW EOUHJFWQI CG WNLWI ECS'F GQYHJFWS WOIYND.

42 ILLUSION SEEING SPOTS?

Stare at the center of the following grid. Do you see little grey spots between the squares?
Are they really there or not?

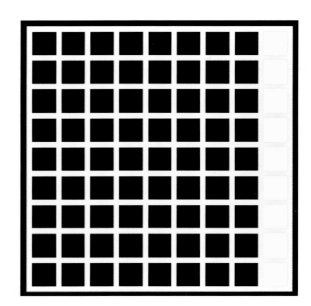

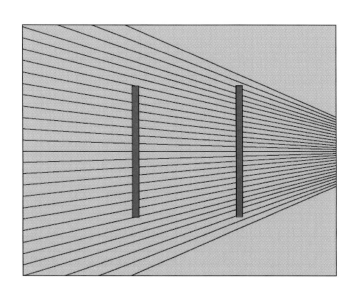

Which vertical bar is longer? The one on the left or the right?

44

PUZZLE   *CRYPTOQUOTE*

HIDEN NEW ABOVG YNVS GI BGLYDTPYBIGL ECITY QNEY YI WI QBYN YNV

XVQVRL, CTY YNVH ERR EADVVW YNEY YNV CVLY YNBGA YI WI QBYN EGHYN-

BGA IGV UBGWL QEL YI NBWV BY. EGW YNVH MGVQ YNV BWVER KREPV.

Do you see a vase of roses or two people staring at each other?

Can you find the secret message hidden in
the two pictures of branches and leaves?

47

PUZZLE

CRYPTOQUOTE

HEY HI STARY, RU UPLOWIUN D NUUL KYENI WZ YRU UDQYR'K UOUPUSYK YW YQDSKPEYU
OUDN TSYW AWON. DSN, OTXU UJUQI DOBRUPTKY HUZWQU DSN KTSBU, RU ZDTOUN.

Can you find a regular five pointed
star in the picture below?

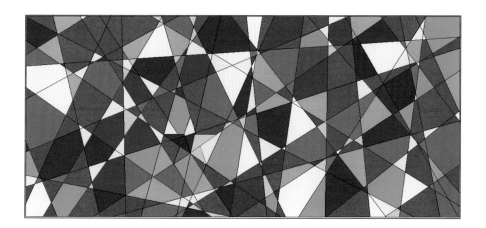

Is this a small cube in
a corner, or a cubic bite
out of a larger cube?

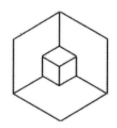

How many arrows do you see in the following shape?

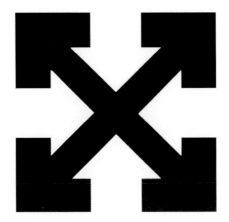

Which of these letters does not belong with the others?

B R P G P

Can you decipher the strange signs to reveal a secret word?

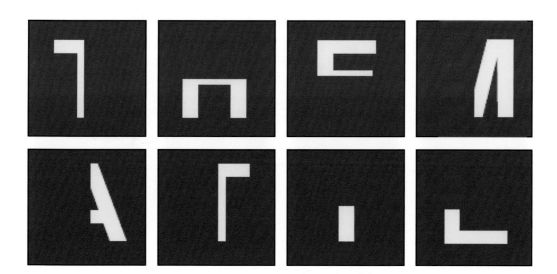

Does the following shape appear to ripple when you move your head from side to side?

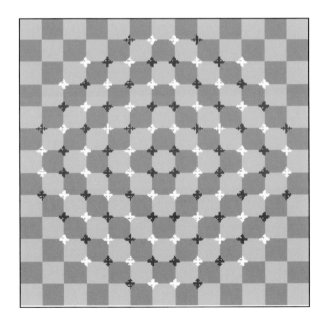

Pick any face card. Imagine that you are shuffling the cards in your mind.

Now, turn the page and the card you picked will vanish.

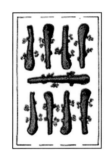

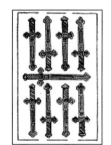

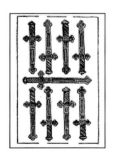

Presto! The card you picked has vanished.

Try it again with another card, if you like? *How did this happen?*

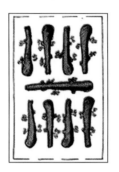

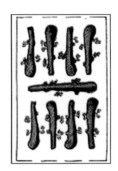

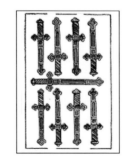

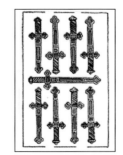

COLOR CONFUSION

Read the color of the letters of the following list of words without making a mistake...

Red Green Yellow Blue Black Blue Yellow Green Orange Yellow Red Black Green Red Orange

WHICH DO YOU SEE?

How many cubes?

5 or 10?

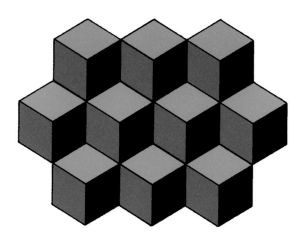

Close your right eye. Look at the spot below and move

the page in and out until the ladybug disappears.

This may take a little trying but the effect is striking.

Where did it go?

O

58 ILLUSION — *DISCEPTIVE RINGS*

Which is bigger? The outer circle on the left or the inner circle on the right?

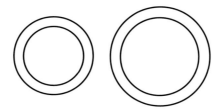

59 PUZZLE — *MÖBIUS STRIP*

This curious surface is called a **MÖBIUS STRIP** named after August Ferdinand Möbius, a nineteenth century German mathematician and astronomer.

Other than the thin edge, how many surfaces does it have?

79

60 PUZZLE — MÖBIUS STRIP

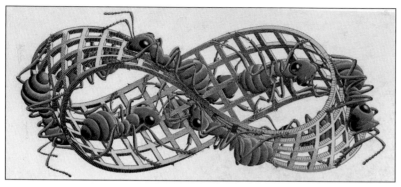

How many pieces would you get if you cut a Möbius Strip along a line running around its center?

61 CRYPTOQUOTE

TRAP SWA ANA ISKKAY

ZWIREMV, VOEBBSMV SMY

YUJEAV. JAEMB UQ S

VUKETSWP YEVOUVETEUM,

TRAP YU KETTKA RSWG.

62 ILLUSION

Is the inner square on the left smaller than the inner square on the right?

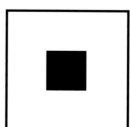 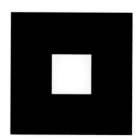

63 PUZZLE — *CRYPTOQUOTE*

MVC GQKIERUAH HYQKWCG NO PKLW MVC AKLMML,
VCQGCG PLK MVC LQI MKCC, ERIC Q HMLKW DELNG,
MCKKRJEC QAQRUHM MVC GQYU HIB.

64 ILLUSION — *ALL THE SAME?*

Which of the following horizontal lines is the longest?

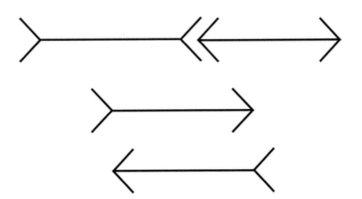

Can you find two secret messages in the picture below?

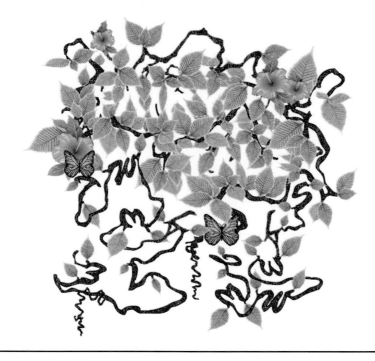

Which line is longer—the vertical line or the horizontal line?

ILLUSION

YOU'LL BE AMAZED

Which square is
darker, A or B?

68

PUZZLE *GEOGRAPHY*

Which states border the greatest number of states?

70

PUZZLE *GEOGRAPHY*

Which state is the farthest north?

69

ILLUSION

**Which is longer, the red section or
the green section?**

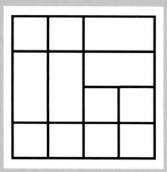

How many squares can you find in the image?

72 PUZZLE

Is it possible to make the following figure? What happens if you cut it lengthwise down the middle?

73 ILLUSION

Which face is in front?

One corner is convex towards you, one is concave. *Which is which?*

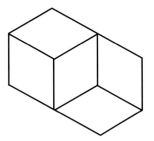

Put the rest of the characters of the alphabet either above or below the line according to the pattern of the previous characters.

A E F H I K L M N T
_____
B C D G J O P Q R

Is this the last slice of pie or is it a whole pie with one slice missing?

77 PUZZLE   *A PLUS SIGN?*

The six puzzle pieces shown below can be combined into a symmetrical plus sign.

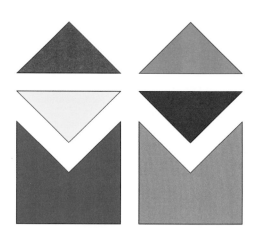

78 PUZZLE   *PATTERNS*

What is the next letter in the following series?   O   T   T   F   F   S   S

79 PUZZLE   *GEOGRAPHY*

Which is the smallest state?

80 PUZZLE — CLASSIC RIDDLES

I never was, am always to be, No one ever saw me, nor ever will,
And yet I am the confidence of all, Who live and breathe on this terrestrial ball.

81 GEOGRAPHY

Which state is the farthest south?

82 CRYPTOQUOTE

LOL YOUR FELF THISHK'I TLBWBON ECTWU
ELW GCMU SCT FEU PURUKI AHF IEU WBW
OCF NHUII RELF FEUD RCHKW FLYU BOI-
FULW - HOFBK FRC WLTYKBONI IFCCW AD
EUT IBWU. LATHQFKD, LI BS CAUDBON L
GCMMLOW, FEU QLBT IUBJUW EUT ELOWI
LOW IFTUFGEUW EUT LTMI RBWU

83 ILLUSION — PARALLEL LINES?

Are the following horizontal
lines parallel?

84 PUZZLE — CRYPTOQUOTE

SKY KITTE INR AYLE WOPK IQGAY QGSSQY RCSK WIRY I KILR, SKLYY-BCONPY QINRGND CN SKY BYR.

85 PUZZLE — VISUAL ILLUSION

Which square is bigger, the blue one or the green one?

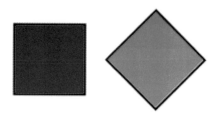

86 PUZZLE — ANAGRAMS

Solve each of the following anagrams to reveal the name of a US city:

NERO   **MEALS**   **SAULT**   **NERVED**   **ORDEAL**
COUNTS   **FREONS**   **TOOLED**   **DIAGNOSE**   **SALVAGES**

87 PUZZLE — *UNUSUAL PARAGRAPH*

This is an unusual paragraph. It looks so ordinary and common. You would think that nothing is wrong with it, and, in fact, nothing is. But it is unusual. Can you find it? Just a quick think should do it. It is not taxing. You should find out without any hints. All that you must know to form your solution is right in front of you. I know if you work at it a bit, it will dawn on you. It's so amazing and so obvious though you can still miss it.

88 PUZZLE — *YOU'LL BE AMAZED*

Can you draw three straight lines that will separate each ant into own area?

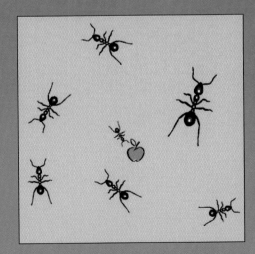

Are the outside rectangle and inside square distorted?

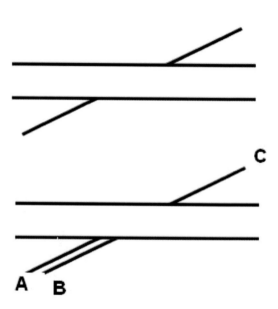

In the first diagram above, the diagonal lines do not appear to line up, but they do. In the bottom diagram, which line A or B extends to line up with C?

Can you find the path for the bee in the lower left of the maze to get to the honey comb in the upper right?

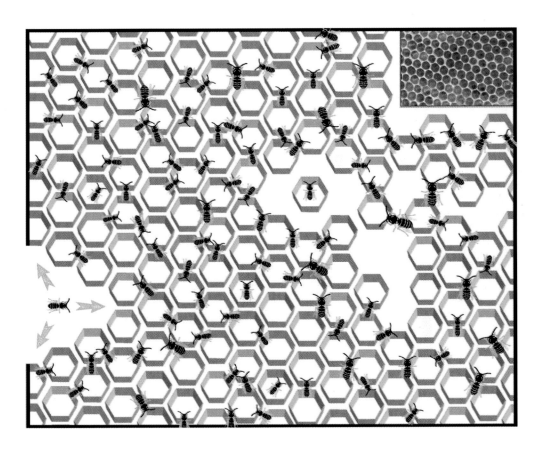

Move your head back and forth. Do the circle and its contents appear to move separately from the horizontal shape?

Can you form two new five letter words from the following?

E R N A G

Which set of orange lines is darker, those on the left or those on the right?

Which mushroom is bigger, the one at the top of the picture or the one at the bottom of the picture?

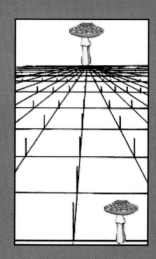

96

ILLUSION

WHO'S TALLEST?

Which man is taller, the one on the left, the one in the middle or the one on the right?

97

ILLUSION

VISUAL DECEPTION

Are the diagonal lines in this picture wavy or straight?

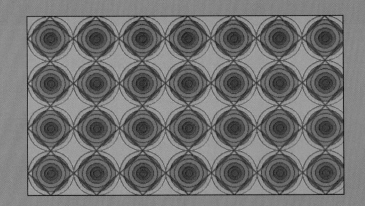

Are the thin lines in this picture circles or are they spiraling toward the center?

99 PUZZLE **CRYPTOQUOTE**

FOUF HEIOF FOLD STLAF OPTYEHI LURO PFOLK RTPSL
UHY, MOETL FOL SFPKG APWKLY YPMH EHFP FOL IKLUF
NPKLSF, FOLD OLUKY LURO PFOLK'S YKLUGS.

NOW YOU'VE SEEN THIS IDEA BEFORE BUT THIS ONE MAY BE HARDER TO EXPLAIN.

One person will disappear – right before your eyes!

1. Note these five gentlemen.

2. We will separate the top half from the bottom.

3. We will exchange the top left and right half.

4. We will combine the top half and reconnect them to the bottom.

5. Presto! One gentleman has disappeared! How?

SOLUTIONS

16 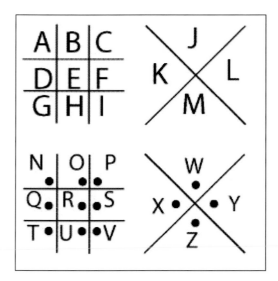 Eight. All three series have 8 as the next element. The first two series are the mirror reflection of each of the first seven integers. If you cover the left half of each element in the series you will see the answer.

17 Alaska

18 'Right before your eyes' is based on the following key:

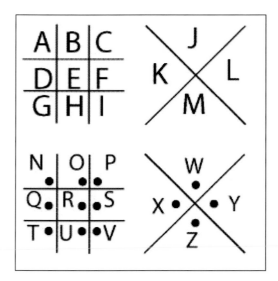

19 Both. Some people see it as a rabbit when viewed one way and a duck when viewed the other way. Let your mind go and you will easily see it both ways.

20 The five boxes are merely realigned into four slightly larger boxes. There were really only four boxes above the line and four below, so when they were realigned they made only four boxes.

21 Pook's ears shot up. Zac had been telling the truth! Trees could talk!

22 The triangle is not really there but the shapes around it fool our mind into thinking that it's there.

23 Cat. You can easily see it if the 'negative' space is filled in. Our minds are trained to see objects, not the space between the objects.

24 Man. This is an old riddle and somewhat of a parable. Man walks on all fours when he is a baby (morning), on two legs as an adult (noon) and on three legs (with his cane) when he is old (dusk).
  (Sorry, I tried to warn you.)

25 Hidden in this book's words and pictures are the clues to the twelve jeweled creatures in the story. If you can find the clues and solve them—and if you believe in Fairies—it will be your story.

26 Thirteen. The Fs are easy to miss in the two occurrences of the word 'of'.

27

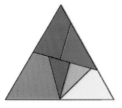

28 Maine.

29 Straight.

30 The Kootenstoopits, who had been warned by Yorah not to do anything at all, sat on the floor and played with bits of the alchemist's tools—copper coils, cork stoppers and shiny glass containers.

31 The bottom edge of the mushroom contains the Morse code message: 'Hidden well'.

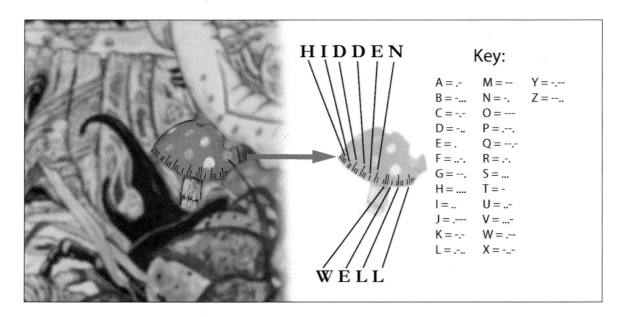

32

Height=eighth
Fringe=finger
Potions=options
Rescue=secure
Slight=lights
Untied=united
Vowels=wolves

33 The decoded sentence is:

Secure options! Eighth finger lights united wolves.

34 Stars.

35 As more thunder rumbled, a flickering shaft of sunlight suddenly pierced the clouds and struck the jewels, making them sparkle and glitter—as if Zac held a handful of stars.

36 Straight.

37 Your mind is trained to focus on one thing, in this case, the black dot, and it is assuming that the whole background is white.

38 This shape is impossible to build with right angles the way that it is drawn.

39

40 Straight.

41 The daughters of Elves don't frighten easily.

42 The spots are not there. Again, our brain is making assumptions about what we see.

43 Both lines are the same length.

44 Yorah had given them no instructions about what to do with the jewels, but they all agreed that the best thing to do with anything one finds was to hide it. And they knew the ideal place.

45 Both. Again, its just a matter of getting used to looking at both the object (the vase) as well as the space around the object (the shape of the two faces).

46 If the two shapes are placed on top of each other they form the following:

47 But by night, he employed a deep study of the earth's elements to transmute lead into gold. And, like every alchemist before and since, he failed.

48

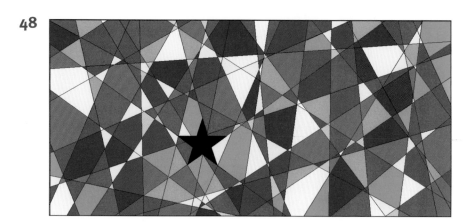

49 Either, it just depends on how you look at it.

50 If you look at just the black arrows, you will see four arrows; if you look at the white space between them, you will see four more.

51 The yellow P does not belong. All of the others are the color of the first character of their name, B for blue, R for red, and so on.

52 Thematic. Each letter is formed from the mirror reflection from the letter in the puzzle.

53 If you move your head slowly, the shape will ripple.

54 If you did this one twice, you shouldn't need an answer – they're all different! But, once again, our mind filtered out everything except what we were focusing on.

55 If this was hard it was because your brain was conflicted between reading the word and looking at the color – both activities we are equally good at.

56 10 or 5 depending on how you view it. Some people see the 10 cubes as follows:

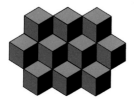

Other people see the 5 cubes highlighted here (turned upside down), sitting in the corners of other incomplete cubes.

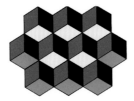

57 This illusion is cause by the lack of visual receptors in the center of the eye where the optic nerve enters the retina. There is actually a tiny spot in the center of your eye where you cannot see. In this case, your brain compensates for this missing information by assuming that the two straight lines are connected.

58 They are the same size.

59 The Möbius strip is a curious shape that has only one surface. Make one and draw a line lengthwise down the middle. It will meet again back where you started.

60 Again, the Möbius Strip's strange geometry will result in only one piece after it is cut down its length.

61 They are eke called Urchins, Spiggans and Dobies. Being of a solitary disposition, they do little harm.

62 Both squares are the same size though the white one looks bigger to most people.

63 The Darklings swarmed up from the grotto, headed for the oak tree, like a storm cloud, terrible against the dawn sky.

64 They are all the same length.

65 The two message are 'Fairy tale' and 'twelve jewels' and are highlighted below:

66 Both lines are the same length.

67 They are the same! I know that its still hard to believe but there are many things fooling your brain here. The squares are gradually different in their shading but your brain it telling you that they are all the same checkered pattern. Also, the light 'A' and the dark 'B' further enhance the illusion.

68 Missouri and Tennessee each border eight states.

69 They are the same length.

70 Alaska.

71 15 squares:

        8 1x1 squares
        4 2x2 squares
        2 3x3 squares
        1 4x4 square.

72 Yes, but it is not a Möbius strip. If it is cut lengthwise down the middle it will form two interlinked rings each like the original.

73 Either. Your brain will flip this around as you are looking at it.

74 Again, the answer is: either.

75 The rest of the alphabet is written with the letters with only straight lines above and letters with curved lines below:

A E F H I K L M N T **V W X Y Z**
_____

B C D G J O P Q R **S U**

76 Either.

77

78 E. For eight. The series is the first character of the name for the integers. One, Two, Three,...

79 Rhode Island.

80 Tomorrow.

81 Hawaii.

82 Ana knew that Rusful's raiding horde had come for the jewels but she did not guess what they would take instead—until two Darklings stood by her side. Abruptly, as if obeying a command, the pair seized her hands and stretched her arms wide.

83 They are Parallel.

84 The happy and very much alive little Doth made a hard, three-bounce landing on the bed.

85 They are the same.

86

Nero=Reno
Meals=Salem
Sault=Tulsa
Nerved=Denver
Ordeal=Laredo
Counts=Tucson
Freons=Fresno
Tooled=Toledo
Diagnose=San Diego
Salvages=Las Vegas

87 There is no 'e' in the paragraph, the most commonly used letter in the English language.

88

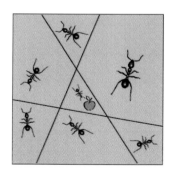

89 Neither rectangle is distorted.

90 A and C connect in a straight line.

91

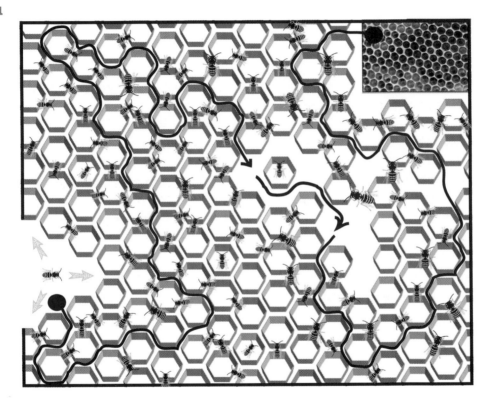

92 For most people, the shapes in the circle seem to move separately from the others.

93 Anger and Range.

94 They are both the same color.

95 They are the same height.

96 They are all the same size.

97 All the diagonal lines are straight.

98 Circles.

99 That night they slept holding each other close and, while the storm poured down into the Great Forest, they heard each other's dreams.

100 This is basically the same as the boxes puzzle used earlier.

This time, the five gentlemen's heads are separated into 2 whole heads and 6 half heads. The whole heads are each combined with another half head, making each one a head and a half. The remaining 4 halves are combined to make 2 new heads. Got it?

Thus, two of the new heads are each a half head bigger in their hair and beard and that's where the missing head is. All of the other swapping is just misdirection.

Acknowledgements

I would like to gratefully thank the following for material used in this book:

The Arabia photographs and information used with permission of Dave Hawley, Arabia Steamboat Museum, 400 Grand Blvd., Kansas City, MO. 64106 816 471-1856   www.1856.com.

Steven Ninichuck for material and photographs on The Beale Cipher.

The Atocha Treasure Company for use of the Atocha Treasure photographs.

The Escher Company Baarn, Holland.

Clipart.com.

FreeStockPhotos.com.

Gettyimages.com.